A Season of Goodwill

10 humorous and heartwarming short stories for Christmas and the festive season

D0776419

Very Large Print

Stefania Hartley

ALSO AVAILABLE AS EBOOK AND SMALLER FONT PAPERBACK

These are edited versions of short stories first published in The People's Friend magazine.

Cover illustration and design by Joseph Witchall

https://josephwitchall.com/

To my family

A SEASON OF GOODWILL

CONTENTS

1 Time for a Break   1

2 A Season of   26
  Goodwill

3 Thirteen at the Table 52

4 A Peace Offering   77

5 Naughty or Nice   104

6 Can We Talk?   129

7 Bogged Down   152

8 A Test of Time   172

9 Snap Happy   193

10 Let's Party!   227

   Other Books   252

   About the Author   258

A SEASON OF GOODWILL

1. TIME FOR A BREAK

Melina poured one last ladleful of white sauce onto the lasagne and sprinkled mozzarella cheese on top. Done. The first course of Christmas Eve's dinner was ready to go into the oven.

The second course—a meat roll made of beef wrapped round mortadella, sausages and cheese—was sitting in a baking tray, securely tied with string.

The side dish—sautéed potatoes and mushrooms with wine and garlic—was resting on the kitchen counter.

She had been working in the kitchen since breakfast, with only a short break for lunch. Now, at half past four, she was very tired. At this rate, by dinnertime, her legs wouldn't be fit to stand on. No wonder every nativity scene had a donkey and an ox: two hardworking animals. Christmas was hard work.

If she were in a nativity scene, she wouldn't be a shepherd or an angel. She'd be a workhorse!

"We're back, Nonna!" her granddaughter called from the door of the flat. She had gone with her grandpa to visit the churches nearby and admire their nativities.

Valentina sat down at the table where Melina was working. "We saw a nativity scene with a pond and a

3

stream! It was real water, running down stones and gurgling!"

"That's nice." Melina opened the oven and lifted the heavy tray of lasagne onto the shelf with a groan.

Her husband, Tanino, came in and sat down at the table, too. "Valentina is right. The nativities were exceptional. One had a cobbler who moved his arm and turned his head. You should have seen it, Melina!"

Melina slammed the oven

door. "You're right: I should have seen it, because I deserve fun at Christmas, too! Instead, I work harder than any other day!"

Silence descended on the kitchen, interrupted only by the ticking of the oven.

Tanino got up from his chair and came towards her with his arms open. "I'm sorry, dear. Why don't you put your feet up?"

"Because the table hasn't been laid and the wine glasses are still in the dresser, unrinsed, and—"

"Valentina and I will deal with it. Won't we, Valentina?" Tanino said, steering Melina towards the kitchen door.

"Yes, we will!" their grandchild agreed enthusiastically.

"But you don't know where anything is..."

By the time Melina had finished listing all the reasons why her husband and Valentina couldn't take over the job, she found herself in the bedroom. Tanino was lowering the blinds. At the sight of her bed, she couldn't resist the urge and flopped down for a rest.

***

Tanino wiped his mouth with the napkin and smiled at the table before him. All his nearest and dearest were there: their daughter, Rosanna, with her family, his brother and sister-in-law, his two aunts and Melina's bachelor cousin, who never missed Christmas with them. Watching them enjoy Melina's delicious meal filled him with pride and pleasure.

He glanced at his wife at the other end of the table, expecting to see her as happy as him. But she wasn't.

She looked like a floor mop. In the last few days, she had worked so hard that she now looked like she would rather be tucked up in bed.

To Tanino's disbelief, Melina got up and began clearing the plates, refusing Rosanna's attempts to help her.

Tanino rushed into the

kitchen. "You have cooked us a delicious meal; you don't have to wash up," he said, slipping his hands into a pair of rubber gloves.

"Leave those! You are needed in the other room to set up the tombola," Melina snapped.

"The tombola can wait," Tanino retorted, though it wasn't entirely true. As things stood, they'd be hard pushed to complete a round of tombola before the midnight mass, but if he were to tackle the washing-up first, there'd be no hope.

"Don't fight or you'll make me more tired," Melina said, unusually admitting weakness.

"Leave the washing-up for tomorrow, then."

"I don't like tombola. I want to hide here in peace. Just go!"

Tanino knew better than to push his wife any further. When she was tired, she was beyond reasoning. He pulled the gloves off his hands and retreated to the dining room.

***

The next morning, Tanino checked on Melina at nine o'clock, but she was still asleep, which confirmed how tired she must have been the night before.

During the mass, she had fallen asleep before the first reading, and hadn't woken up even when the pealing of the midnight bells filled the nave.

Today, Christmas Day, should be quieter for her. Only Rosanna and her family were due to come over to open presents. As they lived downstairs, there was no need to have them staying for lunch.

Tanino went to check the fridge, just in case.

Judging by the amount of uncooked meat and fish on the fridge's shelves, Melina was planning to invite them.

Tanino couldn't bear watching her drive herself into the ground again. It was time he did something.

He padded to the phone and dialled their daughter's number. "Good morning, Rosanna. Merry Christmas! I have a request to make. I was going to suggest we changed today's plans." Tanino suddenly got cold feet. What if Melina was upset about not seeing Rosanna's family today? He'd just have to run the risk. "I want to give your mother a rest and take her on a trip."

"That sounds like a great idea. Don't worry about us. Valentina is engrossed in her new Barbies. She has plenty of presents to keep her busy today. We'll come over

13

tomorrow. It will do her good to stagger the opening of presents."

Tanino breathed out. His plan was falling into place.

He put the meat and the fish in the freezer so that Melina could cook them another day, and began to make them a picnic lunch.

***

Melina opened her eyes slowly. The delicious smell coming from the coffee cup she found by her bedside revived her instantly. She sat up.

"Merry Christmas, dear," Tanino said. "There's a change of plan for today. We're seeing Rosanna's family tomorrow. Today it's just you and me going on an adventure. Dress up warm."

Melina rubbed her eyes. An adventure? "What about lunch?"

"I've prepared a picnic."

"I meant, what about the rump and the bream in the fridge? I was going to cook them today."

"They're in the freezer. You can cook them another time."

While she had been sleeping, Tanino had covered everything. "Where are we going?"

He grinned mysteriously. "It's a surprise."

In the car, as they left Palermo towards the Sicilian west coast, Melina was dying with curiosity, but Tanino's lips were sealed in a well-contented smile.

They took smaller and smaller roads. At one point, a

golden banner stretched between two trees. *Living nativity open today. Next left.*

"Oh, Tanino!" Melina clapped her hands. Yesterday she had complained that Tanino and Valentina had gone nativity sight-seeing without her, but now he was taking her to something better: a living nativity scene!

The road turned into a dirt track that wound up a hill and opened into a little car park halfway up.

A man with a white beard

came towards them with a booklet of tickets. "Welcome to our living nativity scene. Feel free to chat with our actors and take part in the activities."

It was music to Melina's ears. She felt like a child about to enter a fairground. Tanino bought tickets and a map, too.

The nativity scene itself was inside the narrow cave that sliced the rock near the top of the hill, but the path to get to it snaked through an ancient village of cobbled streets and drystone houses.

It was like stepping into the past. Donkeys, goats and chicken roamed the alleys where women kneaded, rolled and pounded grains outside their doors.

Through an open window, Melina saw an old woman making a bobbin lace at the speed of a sewing machine, all the while using her foot to rock a crib that dangled from the ceiling. Through another window, a wicker basket weaver bent reeds as if they were strands of wool. The cheesemaker had a young apprentice who seemed to work as a sampler, too, judging by the crumbs around his lips.

They stopped and talked to the village cobbler, who was very proud to show them how he could make shoes from scratch.

Further up, an old man was repairing a cart's wheel. They stopped to talk to him, too.

"I love taking part in the living nativity show," he told

them. "I admit it's tiring, but I wouldn't miss it for the world. My father and my grandfather repaired carts and they taught me, but when carts were replaced by vans, I had to find another job. At least now, for a few days a year, I get to do what I love."

The village barber saw Tanino and called to him from his door. "Come and sit in my shop and have a free haircut. I've cut the hair of every male villager and I need someone to work on."

Tanino laughed. "I can't keep my wife waiting."

But Melina had already set her eyes on the house opposite, where women were carding and spinning wool. She was dying to have a go. "Go ahead," she told him.

As Tanino took a seat in the barber's shop, Melina scuttled over to the ladies.

The older spinner welcomed her with a toothless smile and offered her the carding brushes. "Would you like to try?"

Melina's reply came out as a squeal.

Brushing the wool fibres and laying them parallel was great fun! Then she tried spinning and enjoyed it so much that, when Tanino came looking for her, she was still going.

After that, they had their picnic outside the inn that had turned Joseph and Mary down, and reached the grotto when it was already dark.

A real-life Baby Jesus was snuggling into his mother. It was such a tender scene that

Melina's eyes filled with tears. "Thank you, Tanino, for taking me here today."

***

Driving back home, Tanino couldn't stop grinning. Despite his initial worries, the trip had been a roaring success. He remembered Melina's excited expression when she was at the spinning wheel.

He had taken his wife on a trip so that she could rest, and she had found work!

"You enjoyed spinning the wool, didn't you?" he asked

24

her.

No answer came from the passenger's seat.

"Melina?"

Tanino glanced her way. Her eyes were closed and a gentle gurgling came from her parted lips. Bless her. His very own Sleeping Beauty must have pricked her finger on the spindle.

No problem. This Prince Charming was going to kiss her as soon as they got home.

2. A SEASON OF GOODWILL

Richard glanced at the paperwork his secretary had put on his desk. It was the proposal for the employees' Christmas bonuses. Was it Christmas already?

Christmas hadn't sneaked up on him in this way back when his son was little and he was still married.

But now that his wife had become his ex-wife, his son was estranged from him and he had no family, if it wasn't for the shops decked out in tinsel and lights, he would hardly notice.

Besides, Christmas made no difference to him. He didn't pay himself a Christmas bonus and he was going to spend the day in his flat watching TV like on any other day.

Actually, not quite like any other day. While all the other days in the year he kept

27

himself busy managing his accountancy firm, flitting between its offices in London, Manchester and Edinburgh, every office was shut at Christmas.

He scanned the sheets on his desk, chose the lowest suggested figures for the bonuses, and signed. A Christmas bonus from the company was an expectation, but there was no need to splash.

He put on his coat, picked up his old leather bag and was

about to leave when a dark-haired girl with a duster in her hand and a vacuum cleaner trailing behind her blocked the threshold.

***

The verb goes first in a question, Michela reminded herself.

Even after one month in the UK, speaking in English still didn't come naturally.

"Hello. Are you leaving?" she asked the old man.

He wore a grey coat that might have been black once,

ill-fitting trousers and a pair of scuffed shoes. Some of the other people in the office wore Armani and Louboutin. He must be the underdog. Her heart went out to him.

"Yes, I am. I haven't seen you before," he said.

"My colleague usually cleans this room, but tonight she's sick off. I mean, off sick," Michela corrected herself.

The shortest words were the hardest to place in a sentence.

"So you're doing her work, too," he said.

"Yes."

Which was a rotten piece of luck, Michela thought bitterly, because tonight they were showing a pantomime at the theatre. She had planned to go with her colleague and share the Friday night buy-one-get-one-free deal. Now she would have to go alone and pay full price.

Well, that was if she could even make it to the theatre, now that she had to do her colleague's work on top of her own!

"Good on you," the man said, and left with a wave, leaving her wondering if "good on you" was the same as "goodbye to you".

His office was clean and tidy and Michela finished quickly. She ran for the bus and managed to catch it.

Upon finding an empty seat, she concluded that it must be her lucky day.

"Hello, again!" the man sitting next to her said. He was the man from the office!

Instead of driving one of the

fancy **BMWs** and **Porsches** parked in the company's car park, he was riding the bus, which only confirmed her suspicions that he wasn't paid as much as the others.

But he clearly was a dedicated employee. He worked late and, judging by the pencil stumps on his desk, he didn't waste the company's money.

"Hi," she said.

"You've finished quickly," he said.

"Thanks to you: your room

was very tidy." An idea flashed across her mind: if she invited him to the theatre, she would pay him back for keeping his room tidy, and she would have company, too. "They're showing a pantomime at the theatre and it's a buy-one-ticket-get-one-free deal. Would you like to be my 'free'?"

He gave her a strange look. She must have been too forward, as usual.

"Sorry, I've put you on the spot, haven't I? That's me

being Italian, but you don't have to say yes, I'll understand—"

"I'd love to come. But I'll pay and you'll take the free ticket."

***

Richard hadn't been to a pantomime since his son was little, and even then, only a couple of times.

In those days, he was still building the company and would work every day. Memories flooded him, laced with sorrow, regret and longing. He missed his son now that they didn't speak to each other.

He shouldn't fall into morose thoughts now that he was in company. The young cleaner had been very kind to invite him out.

"So, what do you think of the pantomime?" he asked her as they walked back to the bus stop.

"It felt a bit like being in a football stadium, with all that whistling, booing and cheering," she replied. "Why did the men dress as women and the women as men when there were clearly enough actors of both sexes?"

He smiled. "Pantos are strange things. They're a very British show. Did you like it?"

"Yes and no. I didn't understand most of what they were saying, which is very discouraging about my English."

"Don't be discouraged. I didn't understand many of the jokes, either."

"Thanks for trying to make me feel better, but the truth is

that my English still isn't good. When I'm at a pub or in a restaurant, I can't understand anything people say. I guess it must be a bit like being deaf. It makes you very lonely."

Richard nodded gravely. He knew very well what it felt like to be lonely. "Would you like to have dinner at my place tomorrow?" he suggested tentatively. "I could cook some British food and help you with your English. There's nowhere quieter than my flat."

She hesitated and he

regretted asking.

Even if she was employed by the cleaning contractor and not by his firm, she might still find it uncomfortable to be too friendly with the company's owner.

He should be satisfied with having spent a pleasant evening out that wasn't work-related. Asking for more was plain greedy.

"Of course, I would understand if you'd rather not," he added quickly.

"I'd love to come over, but

only if you let me share the shopping."

"Deal done."

***

Richard's flat was as tidy, clean and bare as his office. He must be really hard-up to have so few possessions, she thought.

The roast beef he had cooked for her was delicious, as was the rice pudding that followed, but Michela was sad because she was sure that he had grossly undercharged her for her share of the shopping, and she knew that he couldn't afford it. There was only one way to remedy this.

"Next time, I will cook for you. There's just one problem. The kitchen of my shared flat is a health hazard, to put it mildly. So, if you don't mind hosting again..."

"Not at all!"

Every weekend night, they met at his flat. She cooked Sicilian dishes like *bucatini* pasta with sardines and wild fennel, swordfish rolls and *arancine* rice balls, and he made a delicious spread of British puddings.

Holding a conversation with him was easy, as he spoke slowly and clearly and explained everything she didn't understand.

One evening, when he was explaining the rules of the possessive "s", she said, "I must pay you for this. You are giving me English lessons!"

He chuckled.

"I mean it. The going rate for private tuitions is—"

He interrupted her. "If you

paid me for the English help, then I would have to pay you for the company, and there's no price for that. If you hadn't come here tonight, I would have been on my own. All my life I've scrambled up the mountain of success, heading for the top without realising that the higher you go, the fewer people on the path with you. When you do reach the top, you often find yourself alone. Being the owner of the company means that everyone around me is my employee."

Her glass slipped out of her hand, spilling the water on the table. "Your employee?"

His face clouded over. "Didn't you know?"

The man she had believed to be the underdog of the company was...the owner? "I had no idea. But you live in such a small flat."

"I have a flat in every city where I have an office."

"You ride the bus..."

"I don't have my cars with me because I fly between the cities."

"But your clothes..."

"I hate shopping." He smiled.

***

She looked so shocked that he felt guilty about the misunderstanding, even though he hadn't hidden anything from her.

"I'm sorry," he said. He was sorry not to be the person she had thought he was. Would things change between them now that she knew the truth? "You wouldn't have invited me to the pantomime if you had known, would you?"

"No," she said honestly. "But we're friends now, and how rich you are compared to me doesn't matter." She picked up some kitchen paper, mopped the spillage and smiled. "I suppose that, now I've spilled my drink on your dining table, I should invite you to my flat so you can do the same to ours."

This was the last thing he had expected: not only was she not running away from him, but she was inviting him deeper into her life.

"Next Sunday all my flatmates will be away. Are you free to come for lunch? I'll do a spring clean before you arrive."

Next Sunday was Christmas. "Aren't you going home for Christmas?"

"All the flights were sold out. Anyway, I've only been here for a month, it would be silly to go home already. I don't mind being here, now that I have a friend."

Warmth spread across his chest. "I'll be there and I'll

bring some special things."

The next morning, Richard instructed his secretary to increase the employees' Christmas bonuses and to give all the contractors a Christmas tip for their staff.

Then he chose and sent a Christmas hamper to his son, with a card where he said sorry for past hurts and included his phone number.

On Christmas Day, he turned up at Michela's flat with Christmas crackers and taught her how to roast a goose with all the trimmings, then astonished her with a flaming Christmas pudding.

They watched the King's speech together, then played Italian card games and watched old movies, which they paused every time Michela needed a word explained.

When Richard got home that night, his phone rang.

His son's voice was tentative and guarded, but Richard could barely hold back the tears for the joy of hearing his voice again. They arranged to meet up the following weekend.

Back at the office after the Christmas break, his secretary approached him.

"Everybody is very pleased with the generous Christmas bonuses," she whispered.

Richard smiled because, for the first time in years, he felt like he, too, had received a Christmas bonus: a new friend, a rediscovered son, and a whole lot of happiness.

"Good. I am extremely happy

with mine, too."

3. THIRTEEN AT THE TABLE

The aubergine sauce was done, the water for the pasta was boiling and the beef and spinach roll was in the oven. Everything was ready for the family's Christmas meal.

"Is everyone here? Can I drop the pasta in the water?" Maria called from the kitchen.

"Yes, we're all here," Ciro,

her eldest, called back from the dining room without actually checking.

"I'm putting the pasta in the water!" Maria announced to the household, and turned on the timer.

"Oh, Giuseppe isn't here!" Viviana said. She was the youngest of all Maria and Giacomo's children, and she was particularly aware of the danger of being left behind.

"He called and said he's not coming. He's gone down with flu," one of the other siblings explained.

"Poor thing. We must send him food at once!" Maria called from the kitchen.

"Why don't we think about feeding the people who are actually here before we think about those who aren't here?" Ciro demanded.

Viviana started removing the place setting no longer needed at the table, but her brother stopped her.

"Don't, otherwise we'll be thirteen at the table, which brings bad luck." Tano was sensitive to auspiciousness today, because he was intending to announce that he and his girlfriend were getting married. The odds marriages lasting were already bad enough without any extra bad luck poured on top.

"We don't believe in superstitions," Ciro declared.

"I do. We were thirteen at the table when Italy lost against Sweden," Tano answered seriously.

Viviana thought sadly that they wouldn't be thirteen

today if she had finally got a boyfriend, but it certainly wasn't for want of trying.

"We won't be thirteen at the table," Ciro pointed out. "The baby doesn't count."

"Of course she counts!" his wife cried.

"Maybe she can count as half, as she's only small," Ciro conceded.

"If people counted according to their size, those two would be running to roost here," his wife replied, pointing to their enormous fourteen-year-old twin nephews.

Ciro groaned. "Can we eat first and discuss this later? I'm starving."

"We could split the table into two," Tano's girlfriend suggested, so they tried to bring over the small table from the kitchen, but it didn't fit in the room.

"If we sit Brutus at the table, we'll be fourteen," Viviana suggested.

"No. You'll teach him bad habits and I'll never get him off the table again," Maria argued, but the rest of the family thought it was a great idea, so she gave in.

Eventually, Brutus was seated in Giuseppe's place, and Tano hurried to make his announcement before the situation changed.

Everyone cheered, the baby shrieked and the dog barked, and a bottle of bubbly was dug out of the bottom of a cupboard. Viviana reflected that she would soon be the only unmarried one out of all her siblings. It was a sobering thought.

The kitchen timer clamoured for attention.

"The pasta's ready!"

***

Since moving to Italy, Liam had started disliking Sundays and public holidays.

Back in London, Sundays and public holidays were days like any other, with the only difference that he didn't have to work. Shops were open, pedestrians thronged the pavements and cars and buses clogged the roads.

Sundays and public holidays in this small Sicilian town were a different matter: the shops were shut, the pavements were deserted, and everybody was busy with family. And today was the most family-oriented of all public holidays: Christmas.

What was someone without family supposed to do? Plan their lessons for next term, perhaps.

He opened his laptop and started typing the questions he was going to ask his students.

The topic for the lesson was verb tenses. What have you done since last Christmas, what did you do two Christmases ago and what will you do next Christmas?

***

Maria had insisted that Brutus sat next to her at the table so that she could keep him in check, and up until the first course, which was the mushroom pasta, he had been good as gold.

But when the beef roll appeared at the centre of the

table, all thoughts of good behaviour evaporated from Brutus' carnivorous brain. The dog barked and the baby shrieked. The dog swiped at the dish and the baby swiped at her plastic cup. The non-drip cup flew up in the air and exploded. Redcurrant juice sprayed over the table like a blessing.

"Yuck! Baby's juice!" the two teenage boys said, jumping away.

"I said that it wasn't a good idea to have Brutus at the

table!" Maria protested, dabbing the Bruges lace tablecloth with her apron.

"It's cruel to keep Brutus at the table if we're not going to give him anything to eat," Viviana pointed out.

"Fine, then I'll give Brutus some food, but not ours," Maria replied. She had bought the beef at the butcher's and knew how much it cost.

"I'm not having dog food at the table!" her husband protested, thinking of the tins of "Beef and Tripe Delight"

Brutus preferred.

After a short discussion, during which Brutus was being held by the collar, it was agreed that he would be served some of his dog biscuits.

Viviana got up to fetch the biscuits, but the buckle of her belt caught on the Bruges lace and the tablecloth left the table with her.

Crockery crashed onto the floor, glassware shattered on top, and the beef rolled off the serving plate and into Brutus'

mouth.

"The bad luck has already arrived!" someone cried.

***

Liam closed his laptop. He had worked enough for Christmas Day.

He padded to the kitchen to make a cup of tea. Through the thick silence of his flat, he listened to the noises coming through the wall. Next door must be having a lot of excitement.

The kettle boiled and he poured the water into his mug,

then opened the fridge. Where had all the milk gone? Of all days for this to happen, did it have to be on Christmas Day, when even the big supermarket down the road was shut?

The street sellers that perched themselves by the side of the road with their three-wheeled Piaggio Apes only sold bread, salt or fruit—nothing that needed refrigeration—and he couldn't think of a single place where he could buy a carton of milk today.

Maybe he should learn to drink tea with lemon and sugar, like the locals. Maybe another day.

He could ask his neighbours for a drop of milk. It would be a chance to practise his Italian, and he might also find out what all the fun next door was about.

He ran a hand through his hair and tucked his shirt in, then picked up his mug, propped a shoe across the threshold so that he wouldn't be locked out, and crossed the landing.

The din of a barking dog, a shouting baby and the voices of more people than he knew to live there came through the closed door.

He pressed the bell and waited.

***

"The doorbell!"

Silence fell on the room.

"Are you expecting anyone?" Maria asked her husband.

He shrugged.

"Who is it then?"

An unexpected visitor was the last thing she wanted when the tablecloth was mottled with wine, half the crockery and glassware was on the floor, and the beef roll had been gobbled up by Brutus.

"There's only one way to find out," Viviana remarked, already on her way to the door.

***

When the girl opened the door, Liam forgot the sentence he had carefully prepared, the reason he was there, and even his own name.

How could a living thing be so beautiful? If someone had sifted through his dreams and put together a girl for him, they couldn't have done a better job.

She dropped her gaze to the mug in his hands, which reminded him why he was there.

"Hi, I'm Liam, your neighbour." He gestured to his door, spilling tea on the landing, then trying to wipe it off with the sole of his shoe.

He only succeeded to make the rubber squeak. "Could I, er, borrow some milk?"

She smiled and it was as if the sun had risen into the stairwell. "You can't borrow it, but you can have some to keep. Come on in and excuse the mess."

Liam followed her down a corridor that could well have been the throat of a lion, for all he cared.

They entered a kitchen piled with baking trays, pots and colanders.

"Oh no. I've interrupted your family meal," Liam said.

"Don't worry," the girl reassured him. "In fact, you could be just the solution to our problem. Could I ask you a favour?"

"It would be fair, given that I've asked you for milk."

She smiled again and his heart stopped.

"Can you join us for the rest of the meal? We need another person so that we're not thirteen at the table. I know it's only a superstition..." She looked down in embarrassment.

"Of course. It's my pleasure." At that moment, Liam would have given her anything she had asked for.

They left the kitchen and entered a dining room full of people.

"Our neighbour will be the fourteenth at the table," she announced.

Everyone cheered and made space for Liam at the table. He was served a delicious fruit salad, cake and strong coffee that obliterated the need for cups of tea for the rest of the day. Which was good, because it turned out that they had no milk in their fridge, either.

At the end of the meal, the girl—who had introduced herself as Viviana—asked him if she could call on him again the next time they found themselves to be thirteen at the table.

Liam said yes, of course, and she immediately invited him for New Year's Day, leaving Liam to wonder if she already knew that they would be thirteen again or had just decided to invite him anyway.

On New Year's Day, they were fifteen people at the table. If Liam had any doubts about the significance of that, Viviana's warm smiles for him dispelled them.

Now, Sundays and public holidays were his favourite days. He was invited week after week, and one Christmas Day, he and Viviana finally had their own announcement to make, as they, too, were

getting married.

4. A PEACE OFFERING

Don Pericle sat at his desk and looked out of the window.

December wasn't the best month of the year for his gardens—no wisteria blossom, no roses and no hibiscus—but the Sicilian sky was as blue as ever. It made a perfect background for the evergreen palms, dark green bougainvillea and glossy oleander.

He flicked through his diary: there weren't many weddings this month. Good. It meant he had time to prepare for Christmas with the family.

Just then, his phone rang.

"Villa Lingualarga wedding services. Don Pericle speaking."

"Hello, Duke. My fiancée and I would like to book a wedding reception at your villa."

"I'm afraid I'm booked up a year in advance, so if you're

looking for this spring or summer—"

"No. We want a Christmas wedding."

"That's no problem. Which date?"

Don Pericle flicked the pages of next year's diary. November and December were mostly clear.

"The twenty-fifth of December."

"That's Christmas Day."

"Exactly," the man replied. "We're getting married on Christmas Day."

"I'm sorry," Don Pericle apologised. "I don't work on Christmas Day."

"We could use our own wedding organiser and just rent the villa."

"The villa is also my home. I will be celebrating Christmas here with my family," Don Pericle explained.

"We would be happy to factor in the cost for you and your family to spend Christmas away." The man was insistent. "Rome, Paris, London.... Wherever you want."

Goodness, this couple had thought of everything—and clearly had deep pockets. But he didn't want to spend Christmas away from home, no matter how glamorous the location.

"What about the priest or the officiant celebrating the wedding? Surely they won't be available," he tried.

"We've taken care of everything, except for the location for the reception."

Don Pericle bristled. He didn't want to leave his home

at Christmas, no matter how much money they paid him, so his first instinct was to refuse the job. Yet he was intrigued by the couple's insistence on Christmas Day, and curiosity got the better of him.

"We should continue this discussion face-to-face."

***

When a top-of-the-range Porsche 911 parked in Villa Lingualarga's car park, Pericle wasn't surprised. These two had already shown that money wasn't an issue in their lives.

"Nice to meet you, Don Pericle. I'm Giulio and this is Leandra. We are very grateful that you've made time to see us."

"Making time wasn't a problem, but I can't promise that I'll be able to help you," he reminded Giulio.

"Of course."

"Please, follow me."

As he led them down the corridor to his study, Leandra and Giulio commented on the Rococo furniture, the Vito D'Anna frescoes and the

Murano chandeliers. They clearly knew about antiques and art.

He settled them in his study with coffee and a biscuit, then finally asked them the question that had been on his mind since the phone call. "Why do you want to get married on Christmas Day?"

Leandra and Giulio exchanged glances.

"It's a long story," Leandra replied.

"I have time."

They exchanged glances

again, then Leandra gave a little sigh and began.

"It's to do with an old family feud. When I was a child, my grandparents passed away and left all their possessions to my mother and my uncle, to be shared equally. Every single item, from real estate to investments, from the family business to individual pieces of furniture and art, was left to both."

"It sounds fair."

"In theory. But in practice it didn't work: neither Mum nor

Uncle Ernesto owned anything outright, and they had to pay each other off if they wanted to keep anything for themselves. Arguments followed, experts were called in for valuations and the figures quoted by Mum's valuers never matched those quoted by Uncle Ernesto's valuers. Lots of money was spent on lawyers and by the time the last trinket was assigned to one or the other, Mum and Uncle's relationship had completely broken down.

If it wasn't for the fact that they have to work together in the family business, Mum and Uncle Ernesto wouldn't have spoken to each other since," Leandra went on. "I don't want my wedding to be tainted by the family feud. I must invite Uncle Ernesto or it would cause a scandal among the company's staff and investors. But if Uncle comes, Mum will be on edge."

"Are you sure that he wouldn't decline the invite?" Don Pericle asked.

"Uncle Ernesto is very dutiful and he would come because he feels it's his duty to me. But he spends every Christmas in his mountain lodge in the Alps with his family. So if we set the wedding's date on Christmas Day, he will understand that his presence isn't required and will excuse himself," she finished.

"Could this be a chance to heal the rift between him and your mother instead?" Don Pericle suggested.

"No. Neither of them would

make the first move. I don't want to risk it at my wedding. Please, help us, don Pericle."

Pericle thought about it. Yes, he was going to help them, but not in the way they imagined.

"I will," he agreed.

He marked the wedding in his diary on December 25, but only in pencil.

As he led the couple on a tour of the villa, Leandra stopped in front of a marble-topped Rococo console in the dining hall.

"This looks exactly like a

console Mum and Uncle bitterly fought over. My heart sinks every time I see it at Mum's place."

"I'm sorry. I'll make sure to cover it up on your wedding day," he reassured her.

***

If Leandra's mother felt a duty to invite her brother, and he a duty to attend, maybe their relationship wasn't unfixable, Pericle thought as he strolled around the village.

It would be hard, though, and he didn't have the faintest

idea how to do it.

At the top of the road, two village boys, Rocco and Ciro, sat on their bicycles behind a line they had traced on the road with chalk.

They greeted Pericle and he waved back. They looked set for a race and Pericle stopped to watch them.

"Ready, steady..."

Before Rocco said "Go", Ciro's front wheel rolled over the chalk line.

"You're cheating!" Rocco protested.

"I didn't. I just slipped."

They were on a slope and he had clearly let go of the brakes and accidentally rolled forward.

But Rocco didn't look convinced. Ciro rolled back to the start and Rocco counted again, but this time he set off prematurely. Ciro protested and they started arguing. In the end, they both stormed off home.

Pericle had no doubt that Ciro hadn't cheated, but accidentally rolled too far.

Rocco, on the other hand, had jumped the gun because he was convinced that Ciro would cheat. They were both good kids, but even the kindest people behave unreasonably if they felt that they were being short-changed.

Could this be what had happened to Leandra's mother and uncle? Maybe he had the solution!

He immediately turned around and walked briskly back home. He went straight to the dining hall where the

Rococo console stood against a marble panelled wall, with its curvy gilded legs and its pink marble tabletop.

It was beautiful, and he was going to miss it, but if that console could pull two families back together, his sacrifice would be well worth it.

***

Ernesto turned the invitation letter in his hands and read it one more time.

Clearly his niece and his sister had felt the duty to invite him, but did they actually want him to attend? Was this invitation a peace offering or just a formality that he was expected to decline?

He read it again. Goodness, the wedding was on Christmas Day! He would hate to miss out on his family Christmas up at the lodge.

Was this why they had invited him, because they expected him not to come? He was about to toss the card into the wastepaper basket when the doorbell rang.

He opened the door to a

couple of delivery men with an enormous parcel wrapped in blankets.

"A furniture delivery for you."

"There must be a mistake," he replied with a frown. "I'm not expecting any furniture."

"We've been told that it's a gift from Signora Sassi," they explained.

His sister? What could this possibly mean? He let them in at once, and watched with his heart in his mouth as they unwrapped a beautiful marble topped rococo console. He recognised it. It was the one from their parents' house they had fought tooth and nail over.

This was a peace offering. Maybe the wedding invitation was, too. His heart filled with joy.

"Please, come back in a couple of hours to collect another delivery, this time from me to Signora Sassi," he told the men, tipping them generously.

Then he sat at his writing desk and penned a letter for

his sister.

When the men returned, he handed them the letter and a beautiful painting from their parents' house that they had fought over.

***

The wisteria poured its lavish purple blossom over the banister, and the spring sun gave the fresh new foliage a sparkly quality. Spring was in full swing and Villa Lingualarga was at its best.

Pericle watched a radiant bride and groom alight from

their Porsche and walk up the staircase accompanied by birdsong and the cheering of their families.

Pericle was doubly pleased: not only had Leandra and Giulio been united in marriage, but Leandra's mother and uncle had healed their rift and would be sitting next to each other at the high table.

As soon as the waiters started serving the *aperitivo* drinks, he went to greet the newlyweds.

"Don Pericle, your villa is

looking gorgeous today," Leandra said.

Pericle smiled. "I can't take credit for Spring."

"You've done a great job in this room, too. I love the draping, the flowers..., but where is your Rococo console?" Leandra asked.

"I didn't want it to upset you on your wedding day, so I removed it." It wasn't entirely a lie.

A glimmer in her eyes told him that perhaps she knew. "You've gone well beyond duty and expectations. Thank you so much."

"I can't believe that we were thinking of having our wedding on Christmas Day. When we moved it, lots of our guests admitted that they were relieved," Giulio confessed.

"And Uncle Ernesto has invited us all to spend next Christmas at his lodge in the Alps," Leandra added with an extra-sparkly smile.

Pericle guessed that it wasn't just because she was looking forward to a white Christmas.

"I'm very pleased for you."

And he was pleased for himself, too. Without a Christmas wedding, he could savour the day at home with his family.

He walked out onto the terrace and looked out at the gardens. The roses were starting to bloom among pillows of lantana, splashes of blue irises and dustings of tender yellow buttercup oxalis. Bursts of good-humoured laughter wafted out of the dining hall, mingled with the cheerful melody of a mandolin.

Another happy outcome.

5. NAUGHTY OR NICE

Melina always looked forward to her fortnightly haircut at Carmen's salon. Carmen knew exactly how much to trim off and could reliably replicate Melina's favourite haircut every time.

"This year, I'm going to Barbados for Christmas," Carmen told her with a huge grin.

"Good for you," Melina replied politely, even though she had no idea where Barbados was. Could it be a training centre for hairdressers and barbers?

"Unfortunately, it means that I'm going to close the salon for three weeks. Would you like me to cut off a little more this time?"

Melina hated it when her hair grew long enough to tickle her ears, but she also wasn't sure about an extra-short cut.

"I guess that one extra week won't make a lot of difference," she said hopefully.

"I'm sorry, but I'm booked up for the first two weeks after I get back. The soonest I can fit you in is in five weeks' time."

Five weeks was certainly long enough for her hair to reach her ears. "Fine, then give me an extra-short cut today."

Melina watched with trepidation as the jaws of Carmen's scissors snapped at her hair. Even after the hairdryer had done its magic, Melina saw with horror that her hair had shrunk so much that the most prominent feature of her head was now her long, beak-like nose.

Back home, she shared her worries with her husband.

"It's perfectly normal: our noses grow as we age," Tanino told her matter-of-factly.

Did this mean that her nose was going to grow even longer?

That afternoon, as she strolled about the streets of

Palermo with her granddaughter, Valentina, Melina was in a terrible mood. Every passer-by was staring at her nose, every car horn was honking at her, and even the dogs were looking down their muzzles at her.

Valentina, instead, was as cheerful as ever. "Nonna, look! It's Father Christmas!"

Valentina pulled her hand and pointed to a shop where a young man with a fake beard wearing a red and white costume rang a large bell to attract people.

Melina harrumphed. "When I was a child, there were no presents at Christmas and none of this foreign craze about Santa Claus. On the feast of the Epiphany, the Befana brought presents to good children and coal to naughty ones. Now all the shops are full of Santa Clauses and nobody cares about the Befana anymore," she went on.

"Then the Befana shouldn't wait so long to give out her presents, or Father Christmas will always beat her to it," her granddaughter explained candidly.

***

The next day, waiting outside Valentina's school, Melina felt all the other parents' and grandparents' eyes on her nose.

"Nonna, the teacher wants to talk to you," Valentina announced, running down the steps.

Had the teacher heard about her nose?

"Valentina mentioned that

you told her about the Befana, the witch who brings Christmas treats. I agree that we should keep alive our traditions. Given that tomorrow we're having Father Christmas visiting the school, I think that it would be most appropriate for the Befana to visit us too," the teacher remarked.

Melina nodded. "Quite right."

"But I need your help. One of our grandpas is dressing up as Father Christmas, so it would be nice to have one of our grandmas dress up as the Befana. Would you do it?"

The request made perfect sense, and Melina might have even felt honoured by it if it wasn't for the fact that Father Christmas was a benign-looking, ruby-cheeked old man, while the Befana was a ragged witch with a crooked nose. Her nose had to be the reason the teacher had picked her out of all the other grandmas.

"Please, Nonna!" Valentina begged.

"I don't have a Befana costume," Melina snapped.

"You could wear your old skirt that you use only at home, and your green shawl with the holes. They are perfect for the Befana. With a handkerchief on your head no one will see that your hair is short, and your house slippers with the hole in the toe—"

"Fine. I'll do it." Melina interrupted he granddaughter before she pointed out any other ways in which she would make a perfect Befana.

***

Her husband gave her an appraising look and smiled. "You look perfect, my dear."

Was that supposed to be a compliment?

"You need just one last thing." Tanino took the whisk broom she used on the balcony out of the store cupboard and handed it to her. "Now you look the part completely." He kissed her. "Good luck."

"Aren't you driving me to the school? I can't possibly walk on the streets dressed like this," Melina objected.

"I guess the children could spot you walking instead of flying on your broom. I see your point."

That wasn't the point. Her embarrassment was the point.

"I'll drive you," he said.

A few minutes later, Tanino stopped the car right outside the entrance to their block of flats and Melina scuttled inside like a Hollywood star escaping the paparazzi.

When they got to the school, the children were already

queuing outside.

"You can't go in through the main door. Wait in the car and I'll ask one of the teachers to let you in through a fire exit," her husband said.

When Tanino eventually returned, he drove the car round to the back of the school, where Valentina's teacher bundled her in through the fire exit.

"The younger children believe that they're going to see the real Father Christmas and Befana tonight. We mustn't disappoint them," she explained.

Then Melina was ushered backstage of the school's theatre, where a harassed-looking Father Christmas was trying to stick his fake beard in place. Two chairs sat on opposite sides of the stage, decorated with plentiful tinsels and fairy lights.

Next to Father Christmas' chair sat two enormous sacks containing little wrapped presents, one for the boys and one for the girls. Next to

Melina's chair there were three sacks.

"These are the stockings for the boys and these are the stockings for the girls. This, of course, is the coal for the children who have been naughty."

"Am I really going to give out coal?" Melina asked, incredulous.

"Yes. I've explained it to the children, and they're fine with it. Anyway, it's our tradition."

There was nothing she could say to that: tradition was what

Melina had wanted, and tradition was what she was getting.

"Fine," she agreed.

But she was far from fine. How would she know if a child should get coal, a stocking or both? Would the children tell her themselves, like a penitent going to the confessional booth?

No wonder the queue for Santa was three times as long as the queue for the Befana, if she was going to hand out coal. Well, she wasn't going to give coal to anyone.

The first child in the queue was let up onto the stage.

"Hello. Are you the real Befana?" the girl asked.

"Yes," Melina answered, following the teacher's strict instructions.

"But the Befana is very thin, and you are—"

"The Befana has eaten too much recently," Melina interrupted.

The girl studied her a little more. "What's that on your cheek?" the girl asked, pointing to the large wart that Melina had drawn on her cheek with make-up.

"It's a wart, because the Befana is warty."

The little girl's gaze shifted to Melina's nose.

"Right, it's stocking time for you!" Melina hastily declared, thrusting a stocking into the girl's hands before she could start questioning her all-too-real nose.

"Thank you, but I didn't come for the stocking. I came to meet the Befana. Now I know that you are the real Befana. Thank you." The girl rolled onto her tiptoes and gave Melina a kiss on the cheek without the wart.

Melina didn't have time to work out whether she felt honoured or insulted, because the next child had already planted himself before her.

"I've been a little bit good and a little bit bad," he told her immediately, eyeing the bag of coal.

"Never mind. You are forgiven," Melina said, patting

his head.

"I deserve some coal."

"I don't think so." Melina handed him a stocking.

"But I want it!" the child insisted petulantly.

"Maybe you are right: you quite deserve it." She took a lump of coal and plonked it into his stocking.

He immediately pulled it out and licked it.

"It's sugar, I knew it!" he shouted to the other children in the queue.

Of course, how could she not

have realised?

Next thing, half the children in Santa's queue had shifted to the Befana's: everyone wanted a taste of the sugar coal. Melina was worked off her feet and had to start breaking the lumps of coal into smaller pieces to satisfy everyone.

Suddenly, there was a commotion at the other end of the stage.

"He's not Father Christmas!" a child shouted, while the fake Father Christmas struggled to fix his beard back in place.

Some of the children were laughing, others looked horrified, and the poor man had turned red-cheeked just like the Father Christmas of the greeting cards.

More children abandoned his queue and joined Melina's.

Meanwhile, under the heat of the stage lights, Melina was sweating so profusely that she could feel her fake wart losing shape.

"Are you the real Befana?" one child asked after another.

She answered yes to them

all, but what if one of Valentina's friends recognised her and told everyone else? She had to check herself in the mirror.

"The Befana needs a toilet break," she declared.

The children parted helpfully, and one of them handed her her broom in case she needed to go faster.

The mirror confirmed that the wart now looked unconvincingly like a blob of ice cream in the sun. She wiped it off and adjusted the handkerchief on her head. She didn't want to disappoint the children who had come to see the real Befana.

She looked at her nose and smiled. Never in her life had she been more grateful for it.

Back on the stage, the sack of coal had been refilled and some of the gifts from Father Christmas' pile had been moved to hers.

Seeing her return, the queueing children clapped.

***

By the time the school

opened again after the Christmas holidays, Melina's hair had grown back, her nose wasn't centre stage anymore, and she felt a lot prettier.

But as she stood by the school entrance waiting for Valentina and watched the children walk past her without a glance or a glimpse of recognition, she missed the adoring, loving gazes she had received when she was dressed up as an ugly witch with a crooked nose.

6. CAN WE TALK?

Sonia looked out of the window of her apartment. A Christmas tree glittered in front of Palermo's Massimo Theatre, also lit up. The tree's slender Nordic beauty complemented the neoclassical sturdiness of the biggest theatre in Italy.

Palermo was very different

from the Yorkshire village where she had grown up, but after fifty-five Christmases in the Sicilian capital, Sonia was now used to the lack of snow, the noise of motorbikes, and people sipping cappuccinos in open-air cafés rather than nursing a mug of tea by an open fire.

There was one thing, though, which she might never get used to: Christmas without her husband, Gino, who had passed away earlier this year, in the spring.

Weekdays were fine, because her students distracted her, but weekends and public holidays were harder. Christmas was going to be especially difficult.

Italians say, "Christmas with your folks, Easter with whomever you want", so all her friends would be spending the festivities with their families.

Sonia had no close family to spend it with.

The intercom's shrill bell interrupted her reverie and

gave her a spark of excitement: her new student had arrived.

"Fourth floor, on the right," she said into the intercom in Italian.

Butterflies cavorted in her stomach as she stood on the threshold of her flat, waiting for the lift to bring her new student.

The people who came to her to learn English started off being just students and ended up becoming friends. It was inevitable, after spending hours and hours telling her everything about their lives.

In fact, in the first part of a lesson, she explained syntax and grammar, checked homework and set it. But in the second half of their hours together, she asked her students questions to allow them to practise speaking in English.

That was when the friendship happened.

It wasn't an equal friendship, though, and not just because of the age difference between her and her younger students. The imbalance was also in their conversations: she did most of the asking and her students did most of the answering.

So, as they talked about their hobbies, their preferences, their past and future, she learnt everything about them while they learnt nothing about her. They poured their lives before her and she became friend, counsellor, advisor and sometimes even confessor.

Every topic in the textbook had potential for deep conversations.

Even in the first chapter of the textbook, *Introductions and numbers*, the simple question "How old are you?" could foster conversation. Perhaps it was a very delicate matter for a mature student who had turned to plastic surgery to halt the signs of age, or a sign of pride for someone who looked much younger than they were.

"Tell me about your family",

also, could be an emotional quagmire for a student who lived in a blended family.

Sometimes Sonia had asked a student, "What do you do in your spare time?" only to discover that the poor woman barely managed to juggle a family, a full-time job and her English lessons, so didn't have a drop of spare time.

"What did you do last weekend?" she once asked a middle-aged man, practising the past tense.

"I saw my lover," he replied.

Practising the future tense wasn't any safer. "What are you doing next weekend?" Sonia had once asked a child.

"I'm going to stay with my mum, but I don't want to," the sweet nine-year-old who lived with her father replied.

Confessions poured on Sonia's lap, constrained only by the students' ability to express themselves in English. She always received them without judgement, accepting the person even when she didn't condone the actions.

Sometimes, she offered advice, like when she asked a young man who was struggling with the second conditional, "If you met a magical genie and could have any wish, what would you ask?"

"I would ask him to make Marianna fall in love with me," he answered without hesitation.

"Have you ever asked her out?" she said, ditching the conditional tense and the lesson.

"No."

"Then, what are you waiting for?"

He chuckled.

Students poured their hearts out to her and often told her that she was better than a counsellor.

She knew that she could earn more money if she switched careers, but she loved her job too much.

Only sometimes, especially now that she had lost Gino, she wished that there was someone to listen to her, too.

The lift got to her floor. A dapper gentleman about her age fumbled with the handle of the door. She opened it for him.

"It's a tricky door, this one," she said in Italian, then offered her hand. "Sonia."

"Edoardo, pleased to meet you," he said in good English.

When they sat down at her desk, he explained, "I want to improve my English before going to London to spend Christmas with my daughter and her family. My wife had a phobia of flying but, as she passed away last the summer"—he winced a little, showing that the pain was still raw—"I can go on my own now."

Sonia nodded with empathy. She knew the pain he was going through.

"So, I would like to concentrate on speaking. I don't care about reading or writing in English," he said.

***

Lesson after lesson, they spent the full hour in

conversation.

Sometimes Sonia forgot her lesson plan and, instead of asking Edoardo questions that would make him practise this or that grammatical structure, she just asked him what she wanted to know.

She soon learnt all about his family: his only daughter, who had gone to London to study and had never come back, his grandchildren, whose Italian was very shaky, and his English son-in-law.

Edoardo was looking forward

to strolling in Richmond Park—
"such a big park in the middle
of a city!"—and eating mince
pies, which still baffled him for
their lack of meat, despite the
name.

Other times, she ditched the
lesson plans so that he could
tell her what he wanted to tell
her.

Sonia could feel that he
needed to talk about his wife,
and she listened and helped
translate this or that word he
didn't know.

She enjoyed their lessons

more than all her others, and she always looked forward to them. In a short time, they had become good friends.

One day, Edorado gazed intently at the bookshelf behind her. "Is that your husband?" he asked, pointing to her wedding photo.

"Was," she corrected.

"Oh, I'm sorry. So we are in the same situation. How are you coping without him?"

In her many years of teaching, none of her students had ever asked about her.

Sonia told him how she still missed Gino and how she couldn't help feeling cross with him for leaving her behind on this earth, in this city where she had moved to be with him. It was a ridiculous resentment, she said, but Edoardo seemed to understand.

She spoke for such a long time that, when she glanced at the clock, it was already eight in the evening. "I'm sorry I've talked so much about me and taken over your lesson."

"There's nothing you should

be sorry about. It wasn't right that you knew all about me and I didn't know anything about you."

His smile was sweet and tender. It did things to her heart that she hadn't felt for a long time.

Shyly, he lowered his gaze onto his hands clasped on the desk. "But you still know all about my Christmas plans, and I know nothing about yours. May I ask you to tell me about them over dinner at the restaurant downstairs?"

"Telling you my Christmas plans wouldn't take more than a second," Sonia said. She had no plans.

"Then"—a blush bloomed on his cheeks—"would I be too presumptuous to invite you to dinner anyway?"

A frisson ran through her spine. Was this a date, a friendly meal or just the continuation of the lesson? To her surprise, she wouldn't mind if it was the first. "No, you wouldn't."

Travelling together in the lift

was exciting, and leaning on his arm to go down the stairs was exhilaratingly intimate.

All this time, they had always seen each other in her study, sitting at opposite sides of her desk. Now that they were out and about together, the last traces of teacher-student relationship were wiped off.

At the restaurant, they were given a secluded table with romantic low lighting, as if they were a couple on a date.

"You'll have caponata and lasagne," she guessed when

the menus came.

"Correct. You know me so well. Now I want to get to know you, too. For a start, you haven't told me yet about your Christmas plans."

"I haven't got any. I'll be at home on my own," she admitted with a hint of embarrassment. Unfairly, loneliness carried a stigma. She took a sip of her wine.

"Then come with me to London."

Sonia almost choked on her wine. She couldn't think of a

more pleasant way to spend Christmas than with Edoardo and the people she had heard so much about that she felt as if she knew them already.

But it was a crazy idea. "It's very kind of you, but I couldn't accept. Christmas is the most sacred of family times for Italians. 'Christmas with your folks and Easter with whomever you want', as the proverb says," she said.

He reached across the table and took her hand. "Yes, but another proverb says,

'Christmas comes only once a year. Make the most of it while it's here.' For me, this means spending it with you."

7. BOGGED DOWN

Melina loved Palermo, except for one thing: the lack of public toilets.

If the need caught her when she was out and about, her only option was to look for a café.

Unfortunately, the last time she had used a café's toilet— when her daughter was newly potty trained—they had been trapped by a faulty lock. The car mechanic next door had come to rescue her and little Rosanna through the window.

It had been stressful all that time ago, and she couldn't begin to imagine what it would be like if it happened now that she was a grandmother. So she wasn't going to stop by a café. She would wait till she got home.

Fifteen minutes later, Melina was still some way from home and slowing down. The street was uphill and she was carrying a potted plant.

She shouldn't have gone to the city centre to buy a specialty variegated poinsettia to decorate her balcony for Christmas. She should have been content with a standard red one, or she should have asked her husband to take her by car. It was way too far for her to walk, especially carrying the plant.

She had walked that street so many times that it felt as familiar as her own home, but there was not a bathroom she could use.

There must be good money to be made opening pay-as-you-go public toilets, because right now she'd pay anything to use one!

Wasn't there any family, friend or acquaintance living on that street?

Suddenly she remembered. There was someone, but they weren't exactly friends anymore.

Gaetana.

Unpleasant things had been

said, though she couldn't remember what, and she and Gaetana had stopped talking.

They still nodded a polite greeting if they crossed paths, but they tried to avoid it if they could.

Melina still remembered Gaetana's bathroom—pink tiles with a delicate motif of flowers. It was only two doors and a flight of stairs away from her.

She was willing to swallow her pride and ring Gaetana's intercom.

No sooner had her finger pressed the button than she regretted it. How was she going to explain herself to her ex-friend?

Gaetana would think it cheeky of her to turn up out of the blue because she needed the loo. Maybe she should walk away. No. Gaetana's balcony was on the street's side of the building and she would see her walk away. "Let her not be at home," Melina prayed silently.

"Hello?" It was Gaetana's husband.

"Hello. This is Melina."

"Hello, Melina! I'm sorry, but Gaetana is out. Was she supposed to meet you?"

"No. I wasn't expected. I'll go. Thank you."

"She'll be home soon. I'll let you in."

The door buzzed open. There was one less obstacle between her and the Gaetana's bathroom. For an excruciating moment, Melina was tempted to ask Gaetana's husband, but decided against it. What would Gaetana say if she found her not just in her flat, but in her bathroom, too?

"No, thanks," Melina replied. "I have to go."

So Melina set off home, ever more regretting ringing that doorbell.

***

Gaetana was back home later than she expected. She still wasn't entirely used to her new hip.

"Melina came looking for you," her husband told her as she walked through the door.

"Melina? Are you sure it

wasn't someone else?" She hadn't spoken to Melina for months. Things had happened between them, though she couldn't remember what, and they hadn't talked since.

"Positive. I saw her from the balcony, with a plant. She must have heard about your hip operation and come to see how you were."

How sweet of Melina to put aside old grudges in the spirit of Christmas and bring her a get-well plant! She would call Melina to invite her over for coffee, like the good old times.

There was a new spring in Gaetana's step now, and this time it wasn't to do with the new hip.

***

"Hello." It was Melina's husband, Tanino, at the other end of the phone.

"Hello, this is Gaetana. Could I speak to Melina?"

"She's out. Would you like to leave a message?"

"I'd better, or we'll keep missing each other."

"I'll grab pen and paper."

There was the sound of steps, then Tanino returned to the phone. "I'm ready."

"Could you tell her that it was awfully kind of her to visit me. There was no need to bring me anything, she really shouldn't have, and— "

"Sorry, give me a moment. I'm slow to write. OK. *She shouldn't have.*"

"I'd like her to come round for coffee," Gaetana finished.

"I'll let her know," Tanino assured her.

"Thank you."

Gaetana put down the phone and decided to spend the afternoon at home, in case Melina called back.

***

Melina didn't like the variegated poinsettia after all. It had looked great at the florist, surrounded by the common red ones, but on her balcony the white on the red looked like a bird had fouled it.

So she had taken the plant and set off for the shop again. At least this time she would be empty-handed on the way home.

All the same, by the time she got home, she regretted not having asked Tanino for a lift in the car, even if it meant admitting her purchasing mistake.

"Gaetana called," he announced as she stepped through the front door.

Melina's heart jumped into her throat. Gaetana's husband must have passed the message on after all. Was Gaetana still cross with her?

"What did she say?" Melina

asked gingerly.

"I made a note of it." Tanino leafed through Melina's magazines on the couch.

Melina couldn't wait. "Just off the top of your head, what did she say?"

"Something about not missing you"—Tanino continued rummaging—"and that you shouldn't have."

So Gaetana was still cross with her!

"Don't worry about the note. I know all I need to know."

For the next few days, Melina

avoided walking past Gaetana's building, even if it meant a detour with bags full of groceries. Meeting Gaetana in the street after what had happened would be more embarrassing than ever.

***

One afternoon, Melina put her feet up with her favourite magazine.

She was thinking of the chicken broth she would give her daughter when she visited, and of the knitting project she would do with her granddaughter later. For once she wasn't thinking of the Gaetana debacle.

Suddenly, a handwritten sheet of paper fell out of her magazine. It was Tanino's handwriting.

Gaetana says it was kind of you to visit and bring a present. You shouldn't have. Please come for coffee.

Melina ran to the phone and dialled Gaetana's number. She still knew it by heart.

"Hello, Gaetana. I'm so sorry to call you only today, but my husband.... **There was a miscommunication,"** Melina explained.

"Please, don't worry. **Misunderstandings do happen, don't they?"** Gaetana replied **pointedly.**

"Yes, they do."

"And we mustn't let our **friendship be bogged down with resentment, am I right?"** Gaetana added.

"Absolutely," Melina agreed.

"Thank you for making the **first step and visiting me. With a present, too! How did you** know that I have had an operation?" Gaetana asked.

"Well, actually, I didn't," Melina said truthfully.

"Then it was even kinder of you to bring me that nice plant as a Christmas present."

Gaetana's husband must have seen her from his balcony as she walked away with the plant. She was going to have to buy another poinsettia for Gaetana now. Thankfully, the florist down the road had some normal red ones. "My pleasure."

"A variegated poinsettia, too! How did you know that they're my favourite? I've been looking for them everywhere, but with my hip I can't go far at the moment," Gaetana continued, a smile in her voice.

Oh, dear. That meant another trip to the city centre for Melina.

Gaetana went on. "Will you come round for coffee tomorrow?" she asked.

"That would be lovely," Melina replied.

As soon as they finished the

call, Melina slipped on her comfiest shoes, went to the bathroom one last time, then set off for the town centre once again.

8. A TEST OF TIME

Ornella looked down the table and smiled. The lasagne was finished, the panettone was ready to be cut, and her children and their families sat at the table with her for their New Year's Eve dinner.

Her youngest daughter, Giuliana, stroked her hand.

"What's your New Year wish, Mamma?"

"I haven't any. Apart from your father—God rest his soul—I have everything. When I left Sicily to come here, I had nothing. Now I have children, grandchildren and great-grandchildren on the way. What more could I ask for?"

"British citizenship," her eldest, Giorgio, replied from the other end of the table.

"Why? In fifty-five years, I've never needed it."

Today she'd had to look up a lasagne recipe because she'd forgotten how to make bechamel sauce. Surely this proved that she was no longer 100% Italian.

"Things have changed recently," Giorgio pointed out.

"He's right," Giuliana agreed. "We'd feel better if you were a British citizen."

Her siblings murmured their approval.

Ornella nodded. "Fine. Tell me what to do."

***

"One thousand and three hundred pounds?" Her mother looked horrified.

"Don't worry about it: Giorgio is paying. We'll look after everything. All you have to do is take a test," Giuliana explained.

"A blood test?"

"No. It's not a medical test. You'll have to answer questions about British life, culture and history."

"A test like at school? I'm no good at those. I left school in Italy at fourteen and haven't touched a textbook since."

"I'll help you study."

There was nothing Ornella would deny her children. "OK. If you help me."

***

Sitting at the table with a book of sample questions, Ornella's daughter looked like a stern teacher.

"What's the name of the sixth wife of Henry the Eighth?" she asked.

"A sixth wife? Were the parents of these girls mad, letting them marry a man so unfit to be a husband? Why would they do that?"

"Because he was King. Do you remember the name of his sixth wife?"

Despair washed over Ornella. "How can I remember the names of these unfortunate women when I get the names of my own children mixed up?"

"We'll make a mnemonic to help you remember," Giuliana suggested. "The first wife was Catherine of Aragon. Think of a word starting with "C" that you can remember easily."

"Cat."

"Good. Remember that. The second one was Anne Boleyn. Think of a word starting with "A"."

"Alpaca."

Jane Seymour got "jellyfish", Anne of Cleves got "anteater", Catherine Howard was given "camel", and Catherine Parr "crab".

"Can you remember them now?" Giuliana asked her.

Ornella remembered the animals, but there were three starting with "C" and two starting with "A". Which Catherine was "cat" and which was "crab"?

"The man married three Catherines and two Annes! Did

he have no shame?" Ornella cried.

"He didn't care about their names: he just wanted a son." Giuliana sighed. "But you do care about their names, so memorise them."

"Let's move on to another question."

"Which chambers form the UK Parliament? Choose two among: The House of Fraser, The House of Commoners—"

"Correct!" Ornella cried.

"What is?"

"These two."

"The House of Fraser is a shop. Mamma, have you looked at the study guide?"

Ornella twiddled her thumbs nervously in her lap. She'd tried but had fallen asleep before she'd reached the second page. "Some of it. Another question."

"Who started the NHS: Florence Nightingale, St George or Aneurin Bevan?"

"It had to be a kind soul, and most likely a saint. I say St George."

"It was Aneurin Bevan. He was Minister of Health after starting life as a miner," Giuliana informed her mother.

Ornella sighed. "I'm too old for this. Let's forget it."

"You're not too old. Let's have a cup of tea. We can have a biscuit when we've finished." Giuliana winked.

Back when Giuliana was a child and didn't want to study,

Ornella used to bribe her with a biscuit. Ornella smiled at the thought that her daughter was now using the same tactic on her.

***

Giuliana walked into the conservatory with a cup of tea and a biscuit.

Helping her mother study had turned out to be more like coaxing instead. She rubbed her mother's back while she wrote notes, and served her biscuits at the end of each session.

Giuliana sat on the sofa and opened the booklet of sample questions.

"John Constable started the police force. True or False?"

Her mother opened her mouth and was about to form the letter "T", then shook her head. "It's false: he was a painter."

Giuliana smiled. "Well done, Mamma. You've answered a trick question correctly."

Her mother grinned. "I'm ready for the test."

***

The test centre was on the ground floor of a building in the centre of the city. Giorgio drove her there, and Giuliana accompanied her to reception.

"You can do it," Giuliana said, squeezing her hand.

The receptionist asked for her ID and for her to confirm her name and date of birth. Ornella answered.

The receptionist frowned. "Can you confirm your date of birth again?"

Ornella repeated it.

The woman looked at her computer screen. "You are right."

Of course she was. No one could make her doubt her own date of birth!

"I don't know how this happened," the receptionist said apologetically.

"What happened?"

"This test is only required for people under the age of sixty-five. You are older, so you are exempt. The system shouldn't have let you book it."

"Excuse me?" Ornella had spent months trying to persuade Giuliana that she was too old for this test, but now that she was officially declared too old to take the test she felt indignant.

The woman cowered behind her desk. "You don't need to

take the test. You can apply for citizenship without it."

Ornella put her purse on the counter. "I've studied for the test and I'll jolly well take it."

"As you wish, madam."

Ornella was taken to a room full of cubicles with computers. One after another, she answered all the questions without trouble.

At the end, the clerk announced that she had passed.

Ornella left the centre with a smile of triumph and invited her children to a celebratory lunch the following Sunday.

Instead of lasagne, this time she cooked roast beef and Yorkshire puddings.

***

On the morning of New Year's Eve, Ornella was sworn in as a British citizen. Giorgio invited the whole family to the pub to celebrate the New Year and Ornella's citizenship.

"You made it, Mamma!" her children congratulated her.

"I did it only because of you, and I wouldn't have got through it without your help—especially Giuliana's." Ornella patted her daughter's arm.

The pub had organised a quiz to while away the time before midnight.

"What's the name of the sixth wife of Henry the Eight?" the quizmaster called out.

"Catherine Parr, of course," Ornella answered without hesitation.

Her answer was correct, like all the other answers she gave after that, earning a victory for her table.

When midnight struck, they all cheered and toasted the New Year.

"I guess that you don't have any wishes for the New Year, am I right?" Giuliana asked her.

Ornella smiled. "Actually, the University of the Third Age has a British history course that looks very interesting…"

9. SNAP HAPPY

Tiziana caught a glint of excitement in her mother's eyes when she picked up a little red cardboard envelope from under the Christmas tree.

"This one is for the whole family," Emilia trilled, advancing towards her, her whole face alight with expectation.

I guess it's not a new dinner service, then, Tiziana thought ruefully. It was also unlikely to be a kitchen utensil, nor any kind of crockery or linen, which would have been welcome.

Perhaps it was one of the pretty miniature cross-stich pictures her mum loved to make.

But Tiziana's children had different ideas.

"It's a voucher! I want to open it!" Elio shot up from the

sofa.

"I'm opening it!" Corrado shouted, leaping off the sofa to tackle his brother before he could get to the envelope.

"Your mum will open it," Emilia announced, handing the envelope to Tiziana.

"Then it must be a boring one, like a clothes' shop voucher," Elio complained.

"Don't be rude, Elio," Tiziana told him. "Whatever it is, you should be thankful."

"Open it, Mamma!" Corrado was bouncing up and down on his bottom with the anticipation.

Tiziana slipped her nail under the red and gold flap, lifted it, then pulled out a ticket.

It was golden, like the ticket that changed Charlie Bucket's life forever.

Family Portrait voucher. To be redeemed at any of our studios by 7th January.

Tiziana felt the smile she had pasted on her face becoming

more frozen by the second.

A gift voucher for a family photo! It was very sweet of her mum, and a lovely thought, but not at all suitable for her family.

Family photos were for people with children who could sit still long enough to have their photos taken.

They were for husbands and wives who called each other "Honey" and kissed before they went to work.

Family portraits were for

families where the mum and the dad slept snuggled up to each other, kids cooked breakfast for their parents and the dog never made a mess on the floor.

She and Stefano weren't that kind of couple, and their children were definitely not those kinds of children.

Elio and Corrado were sure to pull funny faces, stick their fingers out behind each other's heads and poke each other in the ribs when the photographer asked them to look into the camera.

She and Stefano would stand stiff and tense, as they usually were when around each other. It wasn't even that they had fallen out: as far as Tiziana was aware, neither of them had had an affair, spent money behind the other's back or disagreed with the other over the kids' upbringing.

Their relationship had not been afflicted by any of the dramas that had rocked so many other couples' boats.

But they had grown a little weary of each other day by day.

Whenever Stefano's number appeared on her mobile screen, instead of feeling a little thrill of pleasure, Tiziana's first thought was, "What's the problem now?"

And she was confident that he thought the same when she called him. The communication between them was functional and practical—who's picking up the kids from where, who's cooking tonight—and they never wrote or called each other just to say something nice or to ask how the other was.

But that was normal, wasn't it? Honeymoons weren't meant to last forever.

Tiziana became aware of the others waiting patiently for the family present to be revealed.

"What is it?" Corrado asked.

Tiziana freshened up her smile. "It's a voucher for a

family photo! What a kind thought, Mamma, thank you!"

As she looked up to smile at her mother, Tiziana caught the boys rolling their eyes. Their enthusiasm for the family photo seemed to be no greater than hers.

Well, that voucher would have to disappear in the bottom of a drawer until it was forgotten or expired.

"It's a bit of selfish present," her mum confessed with disarming candour, "because

I'm hoping to get a copy of your family photo. It just struck me that I don't have a nice picture of the four of you. I already have a frame for it."

Oh no. There was no way Tiziana could let the voucher expire in the bottom of a drawer if her mum had already bought a frame for the photo and was eagerly awaiting it.

There was nothing else for it. It seemed they would just have to pull themselves together, make the booking, go to the studio and get that photo done.

***

It didn't start well. The boys refused to put on the shirts and trousers that Tiziana had put out for them, Stefano complained that the studio was too far, and Tiziana realised that she had left her lipstick at home only when they were already halfway there. When they got there, doe-eyed newlyweds and shiny happy families beamed at them from the studio's brightly lit walls.

Just as Tiziana started comparing her family to the ones on the walls, a man with a curly mop of hair and a broad smile popped up from behind the reception desk and thrust his hand out.

"Hi, I'm Davide and I'm going to be your photographer today. Welcome to the studio."

Tiziana squeezed out a polite smile. Elio's hair was sticking out the back like a dodgem antenna, and Corrado must have found the chocolates from last week's party in the car door's pocket, because he had a chocolate moustache.

But before she knew it, Davide had rallied them all into a back room with a huge roll-up white backdrop, a forest of dangling silky white umbrellas and black foam shapes.

It looked like the stage of a minimalist theatre. She wondered if Corrado had chocolate on his fingers, too.

Davide closed the door and, with a big cheerful smile and a whirlwind of instructions, started organising them.

"Boys, please, roll that cylinder over here, push the cubes close to it and sit on them—yes, but sideways, good, yes, rest your leg on it: that's great. Mum and Dad, perch on the cylinder and turn towards each other."

Tiziana awkwardly perched on the cylinder with Stefano, both shifting uncomfortably as they battled for space on a surface too small for two bottoms.

"Move closer, that's it—yes, and a little more—perfect!"

Tiziana found herself pressed against Stefano's side, able to feel the warmth of his body.

"That dangling arm pulls down your shoulder, Dad, and that's good," Davide pointed out. "Place it round Mum's waist. Great job. Smile," Davide went on, but Tiziana was already smiling. When was the last time that Stefano had held her like that? It felt lovely and familiar.

The camera flashed one, two, three times, and Tiziana glanced at Stefano. He was smiling, too, at first tentatively, then more confidently.

Whether it was genuine or not, that smile on Stefano's face made her feel warm inside and she realised that she hadn't seen her husband smile for a long time. Too long.

"Boys, one on each side, rest your hands on your parents' shoulders," Davide instructed.

Corrado's little hand gripped Tiziana's shoulder and she felt the warmth of his childish grip like a delicious tickle. Chocolate fingers? Well, never mind.

The camera flashed again.

"Great job, guys" Davide enthused. "Now I'll count to ten and you'll have to rearrange yourselves into a different position, but still touching each other. One...two..."

"Quick, quick!" The boys were getting right into the game as they switched places.

Stefano pulled Tiziana up onto his knee. She hadn't sat on Stefano's knee for donkey's years.

"...nine, ten!"

From her husband's lap, Tiziana beamed to the camera and the boys framed their parents with their arms.

The camera flashed, one, two, three, four times.

"Good job! Again!"

Before changing position, Tiziana checked Stefano's face. His eyes were sparkling with excitement and he shot her a look of mischievous complicity that made her giggle.

"This is fun!" Corrado shouted, pulling his mum's arm, while Elio and Stefano rearranged the cubes.

The camera flashed again, and this time Tiziana found

herself leaning against Stefano's chest, their hands clasped together, their free arms around each other's shoulders and waists. She was so close to him that the scent of his skin made her dizzy with happy memories.

She felt so happy suddenly that she was almost close to tears. It was as if Stefano had been away on a very long trip and was now back.

"Great. Now I want to get some shots of the boys on

their own," Davide instructed.

Elio and Corrado enthusiastically replaced Tiziana and Stefano on the stool and, as they walked away, Tiziana noticed that Stefano was still holding her hand. With all her heart she hoped that he wouldn't let go.

The boys posed for the camera then finished with a brotherly hug which moistened Tiziana's eyes and stretched Stefano's smile.

"Now, let's have Mum and

Dad on their own," Davide ordered.

Still clasping each other's hands, Tiziana and Stefano perched back on the stool.

"How about you look at each other?" Davide suggested.

Before turning to face Stefano, Tiziana had a moment of trepidation.

What if she found that the magic had been broken, that his smile had fizzled away? Now that she had glimpsed again the spark of loving fun in his eyes, she couldn't bear the thought that the last few camera flashes could break the spell and take everything back to how it had been until just one hour ago.

Tentatively, hopefully, she turned to face her husband. Longing filled his eyes, and she realised immediately from the look on his face that he had missed her, too.

Tiziana couldn't resist. She leant forward and pecked his lips with a kiss. Just then, the camera flashed.

"Great shot! We're done!" Davide declared.

***

After the photo session, Stefano dropped Tiziana off at home and drove on with the boys to their football training.

The memory of Tiziana's scent lingered in his mind, as well as the feel of her skin when they had held hands, her twinkling eyes, and that pretty smile.... He hadn't seen that smile in eons. For a moment, it had felt like having his old Tiziana back.

When they arrived at the pitch, the boys waved at him as they skipped to their coach. That was a first: they usually disappeared without so much as a glance.

Stefano felt touched by that and, instead of whipping his phone out of his pocket and checking his work emails, he stood at the side of the pitch and watched them play. That was a first, too.

Again, his thoughts drifted back to the photo session. It had been unexpected fun, like they hadn't had in ages.

In the last years, even things that were supposed to be fun, like playing football, had become a serious chore. He used to love kicking a ball in the garden with his sons before they started proper training.

An idea flashed through his mind and he whipped out his phone.

Fancy a five-a-side football match next weekend, us and our kids? he typed to his brothers, and sent it.

Before putting his phone away again, he noticed a message from Tiziana. Had he forgotten to do something? Had the kids left something at home? He opened it wearily.

Just to say that I love you. Tiziana xxx

Stefano's heart swelled with surprised happiness, and he immediately typed back, *I love you, too xxx.*

Yes, the photo shoot had shone a light in their eyes and left twinkles of possibilities.

On the way home, he stopped by the bakery to buy Tiziana's favourite cakes, because he had a plan.

As soon as the boys had gone to bed that night, he and Tiziana would sit in the garden with some wine and a cake to watch the sunset together.

***

A parcel arrived in the post.

It was the right shape and Emilia was hopeful that this meant the first stage of her plan had been completed.

Still, she had noticed Tiziana's forced smile when she had thanked her for the voucher at Christmas. It hadn't taken Jessica Fletcher to work out that Tiziana had been less than impressed with the gift. But the fact was that Emilia had been worried about Tiziana and Stefano for a little while now.

She had thought that a family photo, a celebration of their love and what they had created together, would show them what they had and maybe change their perspective a little.

Sometimes she told herself that Tiziana's marriage was none of her business, but then another part of her mind told her that of course it was.

If Tiziana had been physically sick, she would have

done everything she possibly could to help, wouldn't she? So if her marriage was sick...

Of course, marriages didn't always sparkle. It couldn't always be a honeymoon, and infatuation gave way to satisfied contentment.

But something told her Tiziana and Stefano seemed to lack contentment, too.

Since handing over the gift at Christmas, Emilia had kept telling herself not to get her hopes too high about the photo, because there was a very good chance that Tiziana would shove the voucher in a drawer and let it "accidentally" expire.

Emilia took a deep breath and carried the package into the kitchen. She delicately cut the brown paper and peeled it away, aware her heart rate had picked up and was thumping with anticipation.

A glossy, happy family was smiling up at her. Yes, it was Tiziana's family photo!

As Emilia stood up to get the phone to call her daughter, a card fell off her lap on the floor. She picked it up and opened it. It was a thank-you card in Tiziana's handwriting.

The family photoshoot was a great success. It was a fantastic idea. Thank you. XXXX

Emilia smiled up to her ears. It seemed her little plan had worked after all.

10. LET'S PARTY!

One more road to cross and she'd be home. Melina couldn't wait to put down the bags of artichokes, radishes and oranges that were digging into the crooks of her elbows.

She should have taken her shopping trolley but, with cars parked on the pavements, it was quicker to get to the greengrocer without it. The only problem was the weight of the shopping on the way back.

"Is this my beautiful Melina?" a man's voice called behind her.

Who could be addressing her like that? Melina tried to turn around, but her bags were too heavy, so she turned her neck instead.

The owner of the voice overtook her and stopped in front of her. He was about her age, seventy-five at the most,

with a mop of white hair
elegantly combed back and a
dark green Loden coat.

There was something
familiar about him. Was he one
of the doctors she had seen
recently?

"I was right. This is my lovely
Melina!" the man repeated.

He definitely wasn't one of
her doctors.

"Don't you remember your
Vittorio?" he asked.

Memories flooded Melina and
she immediately recognised
the young man's eyes in the

old man's face. "Vittorio!"

He tried to hug her, but her bags got in the way, so he took them from her. "Poor thing, let me help you." He took them from her.

"What's happened to you in all these years?" she asked. "The last I heard was that you became a lawyer."

"That's right. I have my own law firm."

"Good on you! And have you married? Do you have children?" Melina asked.

He grimaced and slapped a

hand over his heart. "How can you ask me this, Melina? It was always you or no one else!"

Melina blushed as she remembered Tanino and Vittorio coming to blows in order to decide who would ask her out.

For a while, Melina had been unsure whether to choose Tanino or Vittorio. Tanino was more devoted and more fun to be with, but he was still a boy. Vittorio was a young man, full of confidence, charm and savoir faire.

"Melina, you can't keep these poor lads hanging on forever for you," her mother used to tell her.

One day the decision became easy: Vittorio announced that he was going to Milan to study, and asked Melina to marry him.

Melina felt like she had been asked to swallow broken glass. She couldn't leave her family, her neighbourhood and..., yes, Tanino. She realised that she loved Tanino, and Vittorio went to Milan on his own.

Eventually, Tanino finished school, got a job in the railways, and they married.

But all these years, she had imagined Vittorio with a wife and children.

"I haven't found a single woman to match you." He sighed.

A frisson of emotion ran down Melina's back. Poor Vittorio.

"How is Tanino?" he asked.

"Very well, thank you. Would you like to come over for

coffee? We live just over there." She pointed to their block of flats.

"I would love to, but I have an appointment with the notary. I'm buying a villa to retire here. You should come to see it. Why don't you and Tanino come to my New Year's party?"

Melina hadn't been to a New Year's party in years. "That's very kind of you. We'll be there," Melina said.

"I really look forward to seeing you." He gave her his

business card, then carried her bags to the entrance of her block of flats, where he handed them to the porter before leaving her with a bow.

The porter put her bags in the lift.

When Melina got to her floor, she rang her doorbell so that Tanino could complete the job without her having to lift a single bag.

Tanino appeared at the door, blinking confusedly. "Have you forgotten your keys?"

"I have heavy bags." She

stood aside and pointed to the lift.

Tanino frowned, then padded out of the door. In his shabby home clothes and slippers, her husband was a far cry from her debonair old suitor in a Loden coat who had left her with a bow.

***

What had happened to Melina? Her bags weren't any heavier than usual and, on past occasions when he had offered to help, she had told him it was quicker to do it herself.

"Guess who I met today," Melina began.

Tanino watched her remove her coat with slow, measured movements. "Your friend who married the baron?" Tanino replied.

Every time Melina came back from visiting her, she acted like a sophisticated lady for a few hours.

"No. You'll never guess."

"Then tell me."

"Vittorio."

Tanino put the shopping

bags down on the floor. "Vittorio Laceca?"

"Yes." Melina grinned.

Tanino closed the front door firmly, as if Vittorio might be just outside. He had been the neighbourhood bully, shamelessly picking on the younger kids, and had given Tanino many a black eye when they were both courting Melina.

For some time, they had been neck and neck for Melina's hand. Even now, Tanino often wondered if

Melina would have chosen him if Vittorio hadn't left Palermo. Perhaps it was better not to know the answer.

"He's back in Palermo, is he?" Tanino asked.

"He's bought a villa and has invited us to a New Year's party there."

"What a cheek!"

"I think it's rather sweet, actually," Melina stated.

A horrible doubt rose in Tanino's head. "Of course, you have turned down the invitation, haven't you?" he asked.

"Why? We haven't any other engagements. I know you dislike him, but aren't you curious to see his villa?"

"Not a jot."

"Well, I am. His party can't be worse than staying at home on our own."

Tanino thought that it jolly well could.

***

New Year's Eve had finally arrived.

Since that chance meeting, Melina hadn't stopped thinking

about Vittorio's thwarted but undying love for her.

Her heart beat faster each time she thought that he was a bachelor because of her.

Day after day, in her mind's eyes Vittorio grew taller, more handsome and more romantic. A tragic Byron-like hero.

The majestic driveway of Vittorio's villa was full of cars when they got there. Tanino had managed to make them late.

"We don't have to stay until midnight if we get too tired,"

Tanino told her as he parked.

Melina clenched her hands in annoyance. "It would be rude to leave early, especially as we have arrived late. You can manage going to bed late for once. Just don't eat too much and you'll be fine."

"No chance of me eating much at all tonight," Tanino said huffily.

Melina shot Tanino a meaningful frown and got out of the car.

A path, lit up with languorous pink lights, led the

eye to the grand entrance of the glittering villa. Music and chatter drifted in the air, and Melina imagined herself on the set of "The Great Gatsby".

How would her life have turned out if she had married Vittorio?

She imagined greeting the guests as the lady of the house, giving orders to the caterers with jewellery jangling at her wrists.

No. She chased the thoughts away.

Vittorio greeted them at the

top of a grand staircase. "Hello, old man! You're not as feisty as I remembered you," he cried, patting Tanino on the shoulder a little too hard.

Tanino's smile was more like a snarl.

The party hall was lit up by large chandeliers, and the sumptuously laid tables were already surrounded by guests.

Vittorio introduced them to the other people at their table and left them.

Melina watched him walk away and imagined his poor

broken heart bleeding at the sight of her on Tanino's arm.

"Is it right that you and Vittorio were childhood friends?" the woman sitting next to Melina asked her.

She was about her age, with expensive hair and even more expensive jewellery.

"More than that, actually," Melina said proudly.

The woman threw her head back and gave a short burst of a laugh. "I see. You are yet another of Vittorio's flames."

Another of Vittorio's flames?

Melina felt offended. "Actually, he proposed to me," she replied.

The woman snorted. "Welcome to the club."

"What do you mean?" Melina asked.

"He's proposed to so many of us that we should start a club. Oh, darling, you don't know him very well, do you?" the woman said, patting Melina's arm condescendingly. "Vittorio is head over heels with every woman in the world. He just loves women. But because he loves us all, he can't stick with one. I broke our engagement because he cheated on me. He's done it with other people, too. He makes you feel special, until you discover that there are many others like you."

Good Heavens, Melina had got Vittorio completely wrong!

She hadn't been the love of his life after all, and he certainly hadn't remained a bachelor because he had been broken-hearted by her rejection. Her gaze swept the room, searching for her old suitor.

He was sitting at a distant table, head cocked, talking to a woman who was giggling. He was clearly flirting with her. What a ladies' man!

Next to Melina, Tanino sat stiffly, jaw clenched in strain as he endured a conversation about shares and government bonds.

Poor Tanino. She had forced him to spend his New Year's Eve in the house of a man who used to wrestle him when he was a boy, all for the love of her. If there was a romantic hero in the room, it was Tanino, not Vittorio. Of course she had chosen to marry him! And if she had to choose again, she would do the same.

"Would you like to go home?" she whispered into his ear.

His face lit up. "As soon as you like."

"Let's go," she said.

They made their excuses and sneaked out of the grand villa.

***

"I'm sorry I cannot give you

a villa like that, Melina," Tanino said as he was driving them home.

"I don't mind, Tanino."

"I wish I was as rich as Vittorio, but it's hard to climb the career ladder without moving around."

"What do you mean?"

"I was offered a management job in our headquarters, back in the day, but I turned it down because it meant moving to Rome and you wouldn't have liked it."

"You turned it down for me?"

Melina was shocked.

He kept his eyes on the road, but felt Melina's tender gaze on him. "Of course, Melina. Because I love you."

The End

Other collections of short stories by Stefania Hartley:

Stars Are Silver:

Is it too late for Melina to learn to drive? Is Don Pericle's vow never to fall in love again still valid after fifty years? Will a falling piano squash Filomena or just shake up her heart? Why does the mother of the bride ask Don Pericle to cancel the wedding?

Fresh from the Sea:

Will Gnà Peppina give her

customers what they need, even if it's more than food? What pleasures can a man indulge in after his wife has put him on a draconian diet? Who will be able to cook dinner for the family with five euros?

Confetti and Lemon Blossom: For Don Pericle, wedding organising is a calling, not just a career. Deep in the Sicilian countryside, between rose gardens and trellised balconies, up marble staircases and across damasked ballrooms, these charming stories unfold: stories of star-crossed love, of comedic misunderstandings and of deep friendships, of love triumphing in the face of adversity.

A Slip of the Tongue:

Will Melina regret faking to be sick to avoid her chores? Can Don Pericle organise a wedding for a groom who doesn't know? Who has stolen the marble pisces from the cathedral's floor?

What's Yours is Mine:

Can Melina give away her husband's possessions because they've always said that 'what's mine is yours and what's yours is mine'? Will the 'Sleep Doctor' deliver on his promises? How will the young Sicilian duke, Pericle, help his friend get married?

Tales from the Parish

Father Okoli dreams of owning a flock of hens and

studying for a PhD, when his bishop saddles him with yet another parish to look after.

But as Father moves to Moreton-on-the-Edge, a farming village in the English Cotswolds, he's plugged into a community of warm-hearted characters, from the motherly parish secretary to her septuagenarian neighbour who's become a cycling champion, and from teenagers requiring driving lessons to atheist publicans who believe in miracles.

As the community pulls together to reopen the village's Electric Picture House, dreams are fulfilled, teen love blossoms and Father Okoli feels that Moreton-on-the-Edge is now home.

ABOUT THE AUTHOR

Also known as The Sicilian Mama, Stefania was born in Sicily and immediately started growing, but not very much.

She left her sunny island after falling head over heels in love with an Englishman, and now she lives in the UK with her husband and their three children.

Having finally learnt English, she's enjoying it so much that she now writes short stories and romance novels. Her short stories have been longlisted for the Mogford Prize for Food and Drink Writing, commended by the Society of Medical Authors, and won other prizes.

If you have enjoyed these stories, please consider leaving a review on Amazon or Goodreads.

If you want to hear when she's releasing a new book, sign up for the newsletter at:

www.stefaniahartley.com/subscribe You'll also receive an exclusive short story.